Foreword

It has been a real pleasure getting to know Coy's never-ending perspective and sense of humor. Amy Giggles is a great portrayal of a child's journey through acceptance among peers and overcoming social challenges while maintaining and holding onto what makes us all special. Sometimes kids can be cruel. Before they realize it, they can create hurt feelings and cause insecurities within other children. We may spend our whole lives trying to fix what happens to us when we are young. The blessed people can maintain their identity through a sea of ridicule and a world that will tell you that you will never get to your dreams. I encourage you to be like Amy Giggles and always fight to keep your laughter, imagination and your light out of the wind and cold. Coy has his inner child preserved safely under his fedora. Please enjoy this spark of his imagination and there will be many Giggles to come.

-Zac Brown

There once was
a girl named
AMY GIGGLES.

She loved
to laugh, and
she loved
to be tickled.

Like a singing pink rhino
or a dancing blue bunny.

People made fun
of her loud, lovely
laugh. They said, "You
laugh too loud ~ you
should cut it in half."

"You sound
like a donkey,
and you look
like a clown.
Oh please,
oh please!
Won't you please
quiet down?"

Everyone would point and be so mean. She told her family about making a scene. Her mother told her it would be all right. "Just eat your dinner and have a good night." Her father said, "Amy, you laugh just fine. Those meanies don't matter ~ don't you pay them no mind."

She went to her room and made a stand. "I'm AMY GIGGLES, and I'll never laugh again! When things are funny, I'll hold it all in. Never, Oh Ever, will I ever laugh again."

"If I see a big dog driving a boat, a cat that can count or a rock that floats... If I stumble on a possum riding a whale... I say to my laugh, 'Laugh, farewell!'"

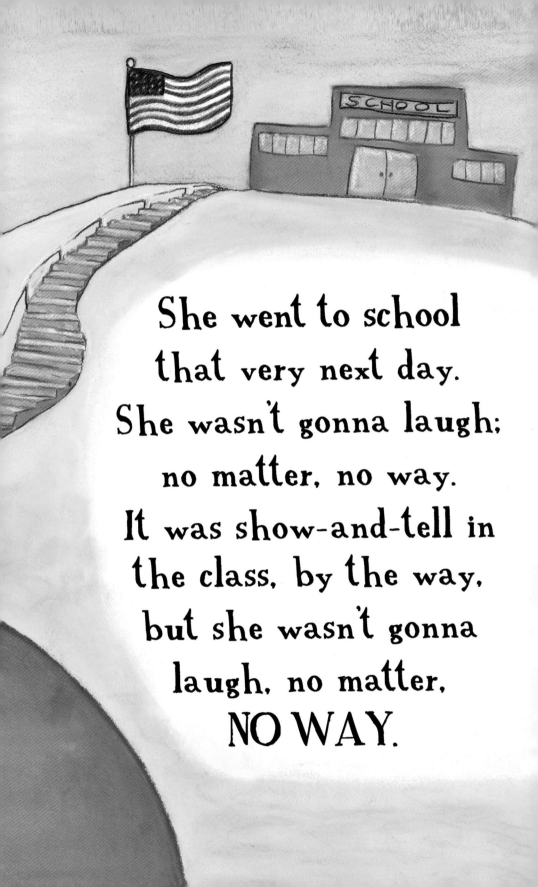

She went to school
that very next day.
She wasn't gonna laugh;
no matter, no way.
It was show-and-tell in
the class, by the way,
but she wasn't gonna
laugh, no matter,
NO WAY.

There was a fish, and a
hammer, and even a tent. The room
was loud and full of excitement.

A frog made noises and everyone giggled. But not AMY GIGGLES, her toes just wiggled.

When things were funny, her nose would snort. She'd huff and puff, and her face would distort.

She held it all in so she wouldn't be a bother, but she sounded like an elephant breathing underwater.

"I'll snort through my nose. I'll huff and puff and wiggle my toes. Even if it's or my very best friend, my name is AMY GIGGLES and I'll never laugh again."

During lunch, the frog got loose. Amy had no clue ~ she was drinking her juice.

It landed in her lap and
she started to blow.
AMY GIGGLES shot juice
to and fro.

The juice was loose. All were slipping and sliding. The frog was hopping and the kids were all hiding. They all started screaming and carrying on.

Amy tried to hold
it in, but she couldn't
for long.

The frog and the juice were just too much.

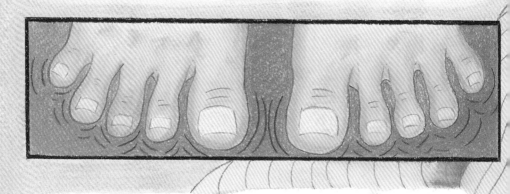

She had to laugh or she would just bust.

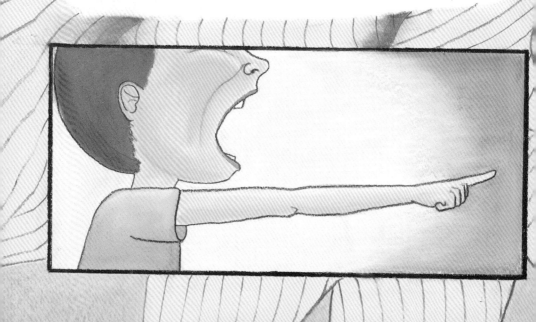

She huffed and puffed and wiggled her toes. Her friend screamed, "She's about to explode!"

She snorted and tried to hold it all in, but there was...

AND THEN A
GRIN

She chuckled and giggled at all the commotion.

Everyone knew this must be insane. Amy Giggles had said she'd never laugh again.

Her laugh was loud, and even contagious. They all started laughing and being outrageous. Her classmates thought she was special and sweet. They all laughed louder because she was so unique. She said, "My name is AMY GIGGLES, and I'll never care what people say AGAIN!"

"I LIKE MY LAUGH AND I'LL NEVER HOLD IT IN!"

About the Author

Coy Bowles is a writer, musician, member of the three-time Grammy Award-winning Zac Brown Band, & his own band, Coy Bowles & the Fellowship. Coy Bowles is a co-writer of many of Zac Brown Band's songs including the #1 hit singles "Colder Weather," "Knee Deep" & "Sweet Annie." Bowles taught music for over a decade prior to joining Zac Brown Band, & the experiences garnered while working with children inspired him to become a writer. Bowles has a fundamental belief that encouraging children to achieve their dreams can change their lives forever. He is from Thomaston, Georgia and is a graduate of Georgia State University with a degree in music.

A Note from Coy

A fellow named Donnie McCormick took me under his wing when I was young and taught me the true nature of creativity. He was a poet, painter, songwriter, and musician. When Donnie passed away, I learned that people you love and admire never leave you, even when their time for another existence comes. Every time I write a song, I ask myself if he would like it. He is still with me. As a tribute to my friend, I promised myself to be creative in as many areas as my life would allow. Life continued and I met a girl who told me the story of how she had been made fun of because of her laugh. She told me how she had changed her laugh into a "huffing, puffing" sound in order to stop the teasing. I was amazed that one would change themselves due to ridicule. From her story, I was inspired to write Amy Giggles ~ Laugh Out Loud. Two years, and many hours of work later, my creative writing project came together. I hope it inspires you...Enjoy!